Death by Deception

A Murder By Misdirection Prequel

Debra Snow

MIND
BENDER
PRESS

Cover Design: Marianne Nowicki, PremadeEbookCoverShop.com

ISBN13: ISBN: 978-1737838173

Published by:
Mindbender Press
474 South Main Street
Phillipsburg NJ 08865
www.mindbenderpress.com

Dedication

To Kathy

"There is nothing more deceptive than an obvious fact."

— *Arthur Conan Doyle*

"The art of pleasing is the art of deception."
— *Luc de Clapiers*

1. The Pledge

The police car came to a stop in front of the building on West 56th Street. Two uniformed officers stepped quickly out. The driver was a lanky African-American man with graying hair and a bit of a belly. He rose to his full height of six feet and fixed his dark brown eyes on the building.

Out of the passenger side came a striking young African-American woman with her hair pulled back and under her hat. She was almost as tall as her partner, and despite her caramel-colored skin tone, her eyes were a bright, clear blue.

Since it was summer, they both had their arms exposed by the short-sleeved uniform shirts they wore. They had equipment belts with handcuffs, magazines, and other necessities. They also held nightsticks and their service weapons holstered by their sides.

The pair stepped under the green awning and through the door of the large apartment building.

A thin young man in a dark brown suit a size too big met them in the hall.

"Thank God you're here," he spoke quietly but with fear.

"Where is the…uh…situation?" the older officer asked.

"Right this way, please," he muttered and led them down the hall.

"You okay, Pro?" the man said to his partner.

"One hundred percent, Terrell," Prophecy Thompson shot back, glancing at him with her amazing eyes.

Terrell Hodges gave a nod back. He liked the rookie. She was indeed a pro, and her nickname suited her. Working with her for almost a year, he'd learned that with her by his side, they could walk into anything and it would turn out all right.

They moved down a hall and Pro kept up, but Terrell panted from the pace.

"How big is this place?" Pro muttered.

"Big!" responded Terrell, who whooshed in another breath. "How much further, buddy?"

The young security officer slowed his step. "Just a little further, sir."

"Are these all apartments?" Terrell wheezed.

"Condos, sir. The whole place went condo years ago."

"Of course they did," Terrell muttered, and gave a telling look to his partner.

They arrived at a door in the back of the building, and the brown-suited man pulled out a large ring of keys. "I'm afraid it's not very nice," he apologized. "No one had seen him for days, and when I went in this morning…"

He closed his eyes and gave a shudder.

"Just unlock the door, then go back and lead any other officers back here when they arrive," Terrell told him.

Pro had already pulled latex gloves from her pocket and was putting them on to her hands one at a time.

Terrell watched as the younger man went through the keys. Pro offered gloves to her partner and a small canister of menthol gel.

He rubbed the mentholated ointment under his nose, and pulled on the first glove as he grunted a quick, "Thank you."

The officers stepped into the room, and the menthol gel only partially blocked the smell that hit them. Neither had pulled their weapon, as there was no threat, just a dead body.

The apartment was small, obviously one of the less-expensive condominiums in the building. Bookcases lined the walls, each one with dusty books and thin pamphlets. But there were also little boxes and silk handkerchiefs on several shelves. One shelf was nothing but packs of playing cards of different colors and some with strange white wrappers around them.

"This guy was a magician," Pro stated plainly to her partner as they moved through the small living room/kitchen towards the bedroom.

"Huh?" Terrell answered with a frown. "What makes you think that?"

"Look at the things on the shelves," Pro said and pointed around the room. "There are props everywhere and an extensive collection of magic books!"

"You can read the titles from here?" Terrell marveled in a quiet tone.

"No, I just recognize them," Pro answered.

They stepped through the bedroom door, and there was the victim.

There was no doubt it was murder. The tall, Caucasian man sat on the floor with his back leaning against the bed. He had curly black hair and several tattoos on his exposed arms. He wore a black T-shirt and black pants. The most obvious item was the fanciful hilt of what was undoubtedly a knife standing out at a sickening angle from his chest. The knife had an odd hilt, with a circular opening at the end, like a large ring.

There was a small puddle of blood on the maroon comforter on top of the bed, but little on the floor.

Pro cleared her throat. "I guess we need to call Homicide."

"You think?" Terrell smirked, pulled his cell phone and looked at the screen. "I gotta call from the hall. You okay here alone with the DB?"

Pro gave a nod, recognizing the abbreviation for 'dead body.' "Yes, it gives me a chance to observe the scene."

"But you know…?"

"I know, don't touch anything," Pro sighed.

Terrell gave her a smile. "I taught you good, kid."

"You taught me *well*, Terrell," Pro corrected.

"I know, I just said that. But I'm glad you agree," Terrell jibed and stepped out into the hallway.

As the older man left, Pro noted something covered with a decorative cloth next to the closet in the room's corner. It was taller than her, wider than the closet door, and shoved into the corner. She walked over to peek at it.

The cloth that covered it was some kind of East India design, with a gold thread weaved into the multi-colored tapestry. She pulled it aside to see that it covered a full sheet of plywood, four feet wide and eight feet tall and at least a full inch thick. A large frame of two by four lumber supported the panel on the side that faced away from the door.

Pro gently removed the cloth completely and noted that marks covered the surface of the board. The indentations were thin and came at all different angles, and Pro thought it appeared as if someone had taken a hammer and wood chisel to the plywood. She also noted that the marks were mostly on the outer area of the board, while the center was undamaged.

She put the cover back into place and waited for her partner to return.

Two detectives arrived shortly, which didn't surprise Pro, as they were a mere two blocks from their precinct. They looked familiar as they all worked in the same building, but Pro didn't know their names.

One was an average-height Asian man with a thin build and a full head of dark hair. Pro noted he moved with confidence and grace. The second detective, his partner, was a white-haired Caucasian man with the face of a bulldog, who glowered at the crimes scene as if he'd seen one too many of them.

The Asian man spoke first. "Officer, is the scene secure?"

He spoke with no accent, and Pro noticed he didn't even have the sound of a local region in his voice.

"Yes, detective," Pro responded. "My partner is watching the hallway, and I've been here with the DB since we arrived."

"Aw, geez, this one is a stinker," the older detective cursed.

Pro quickly retrieved her small container of menthol ointment and offered it. The white-haired man looked at the young woman with eyes that seemed to not have gotten enough sleep in twenty years. He took it from her, scooped his finger through it, and applied it under his nose.

Pro offered it to the other, who also took some, smiled and said, "You're very prepared, officer—?"

"Thompson, sir. Pro Thompson."

The older man cleared his throat. "Is that your name, or a nickname?"

"It's short for Prophecy, sir," Pro explained. "My father had some funny ideas."

"I like it," the Asian detective told her. "It has character. I'm Detective Chu."

He offered his hand, and Pro shook it.

"And I'm Franks," his partner offered, also shaking hands. "What can you tell us, officer?"

Pro brightened. "Well, cause of death obvious—"

"You mean the knife sticking out of his chest?" Franks joked.

"Yes, sir. However, someone could have stabbed him with it post mortem."

Chu interrupted. "Why do you think that, officer?"

"Blood, sir. I would expect there would be a lot more blood here on the floor. However, he could have been stabbed and fallen on the bed and then slid down to the floor, so the blood would have pooled and absorbed by the bedding." She pointed at a stain on top of the comforter. "Robbery wasn't a motive, as his wallet was sitting out there on the table." She pointed at a nearby bureau. "However, I haven't seen his cell phone, and I don't see the shape of one in his pockets."

"What if it's in his back pocket?" Franks suggested.

Chu looked worried. "You didn't move the body, did you?"

"No, sir, that would be against protocol until forensics gets here. It *might* be in his back pocket, but since I haven't seen his phone, that would be the first thing I would try to find."

The two detectives watched her, and Pro suddenly felt uncomfortable. Finally, she muttered, "I mean, if I were working the scene."

Franks looked pleased. "Anything else, officer?"

"The vic appears to have been a magician, but I'm not sure if he was amateur or professional."

"Okay, now how the heck do you know that, officer?" Franks demanded.

Chu broke in. "The things around the place. Didn't you see them when we came in? Those silks and props on the bookshelves?"

Franks raised his hands in a pose of surrender. "I'll step back and let you hotshots take it. I'll find out when forensics is going to get here."

He exited the room while pulling out his cell phone. Chu pulled out gloves and put them on.

"I see you gloved up as well," Chu noted, his eyes on Pro's hands.

"Yes, sir."

"And you also brought the menthol stuff. Do you get called in to many homicides?"

Pro flushed a little. "To be honest, detective, this is my first one."

Chu nodded. "Really? Well, good call on the blood pooling, the phone, and the magic props. How long have you been on the job?"

"One year, sir."

Chu raised an eyebrow. "A rookie?"

"I guess, sir."

"What's your background?"

"College grad, master's degree in science."

"Master's degree? Impressive. So why didn't you go into forensics?"

Pro gave a heavy sigh. "My dad was a beat cop. He passed on about six months ago."

"On the job?"

"No sir, cancer," Pro said, unable to meet his eyes.

"That's rough."

She lifted her head. "Seeing me graduate the police academy was the proudest day of his life, sir."

Chu couldn't help but smile. "I bet it was Officer Thompson. I bet it was."

Franks came back into the bedroom. "I see you gloved up. You needn't have bothered. The Crime Scene Unit is coming in now, and they are throwing us all out until they finish the preliminary."

Pro's back became straighter. "I'll help my partner secure the scene, detective."

She headed out of the room as the two men watched her go.

"She's observant, smart," Franks mused. "Got a good head on her shoulders."

"That's true," Chu replied.

"You know, I'm retiring in about a month—"

"Do you have to remind me?"

"Maybe it's time for *you* to be the senior partner."

Chu shook his head. "She's only been on the job a year. She won't even finish her probation for another six months. That's too green."

"How long were you on the job before I pulled you out of that uniform?"

"Three years."

Franks chuckled. "Maybe she's just three times better than you."

The detectives moved out of the bedroom as the team of forensic officers came into the small apartment.

Pro sat next to her partner in their police cruiser. Terrell typed away on the keyboard of their mobile computer that was attached to a metal panel with a spring loaded movable arm. It turned so either of them could use it and secure it when they drove.

Meanwhile, Pro made notes in a small notebook she had pulled from her pocket.

"Why do you always do that?" Terrell goaded.

"Hmm?" Pro said and looked up.

"You afraid the reports I write aren't up to snuff?"

"Of course they are," Pro smirked and went back to writing. "You're just the world's worst typist."

"Officer Thompson, it would really annoy me if that weren't true!"

"Officer Hodges, your reports are fine once I review them."

"There's teamwork for you."

She looked up from the notebook again. "I make notes to help my memory. I like to write things down while they're fresh in my mind."

"Don't know why you bother. Our part in this is done. It's up to the detectives now."

"Then it's good practice for when I'm a detective," Pro insisted.

Terrell gave a quick laugh. "That's you, Pro, always looking ahead."

She closed her notebook and looked at her partner. "Besides, I think I knew this guy."

"Our DB? How?"

"I think I saw him perform or something. I believe he was a busker."

"A what?" Terrell frowned at the unfamiliar term.

"A street-magician."

"You mean like David Blaine? I love that guy."

"I might do a little investigating on this myself."

"Oh, man," Terrell grumbled. "There you go again, Pro."

"What?"

"Driving all over the city, chasing down perps ain't keeping you busy enough? You haveta find more work for yourself."

"It's all right. I'll do it when I'm off duty."

Terrell shook his head as he finished typing. "You need to get a boyfriend, Pro."

Pro gave him a look. "Says the old married guy? You haven't dated in this century, Hodges."

"Hey, at my wedding we partied like it was 1999."

"That's because it *was* 1999."

Terrell considered this. "And a great party it was. Look, Pro, my kids are in college, and these days, my wife and I get to relax."

"Yeah, at home, because all your money is paying for your kids to go to college."

"I can't argue with that," Terrell chuckled.

"You don't have a clue what the dating scene is like these days. I have no interest."

Terrell finished and pivoted the metal arm so that the computer faced Pro. "So, since you aren't dating, check the report and make sure I typed good."

"Typed well," Pro corrected and focused on the screen.

A female voice came over the radio. "Car 54, Car 54, this is dispatch."

Terrell grabbed the microphone from its holder on the dash and spoke. "This is car 54, over."

"We have a 10-64-N at Broadway and 52nd Street. Repeat, a 10-64-N at Broadway and 52nd Street."

"We're on it, over," Terrell replied, and started the car. He hung the microphone on its hook and put the car into gear.

"Great, a panhandler," Pro grumbled. "Is that all?"

"Can't stay here, Pro. They got more than enough people at this scene. They don't need us. Can you type while I drive?"

"Yes, go."

Terrell pulled the car up the street and headed down the block towards Broadway. They cruised slowly through the Manhattan traffic. They hadn't set off the lights or siren as it was not an emergency, just a panhandler that needed to be moved. Of course, some panhandlers and homeless could get aggressive, so it was best to take the situation seriously.

"Mick Wexler?" Pro said aloud as she read the screen.

"Yes, that's the DB. I checked with the doorman, or security, or whatever that guy was."

"He was security, his name was Jonas Blake," Pro frowned. "But the DB, Wexler. I *have* heard his name before."

Terrell was facing straight ahead, his eyes on the road. "You a fan of magic?"

Pro made a face like she tasted something bad. "No, but I know people who are."

"How?"

Pro stayed focused on her typing, and just grunted, "I hear things…around…"

As the police cruiser pulled on to Broadway and headed downtown, Terrell seemed alarmed.

"What is it?" Pro asked, concerned by her partner's reaction.

"Looks like there's quite a crowd there," Terrell worried.

Pro looked down the street, and he'd been right. People were crowding the sidewalk and not going anywhere. This was not a safe situation, and Pro and Terrell knew it was a place where pickpockets and purse-snatchers could work their trades.

Terrell put on the flashing lights, but not the siren, as he didn't want to scare people, and pulled to the curb.

They stepped onto the street, and in front of them was a large open space known as Paramount Plaza. They named it for the many-storied Paramount building which towered over the space. The sidewalk was much wider, and it led to a raised area reached by climbing three long steps that ran across the entire front. Pro could see large planters filled with bright flowers and benches where people could sit. They covered all of it, the pavement, planters, and benches, with a shiny black stone

On one bench in the center of the crowd, there stood a red-headed young man with a short, tightly cropped beard. He wore formal pants and a light green shirt, with a green plaid vest of wool. On his head, he wore a rounded flat cap of the same fabric as the vest with a small stiff brim in front, like a newspaper boy from a hundred years earlier. He had a small wireless microphone on his ears, which had a stiff wire that looped around in front of his face. He also wore a small speaker on his belt that amplified his voice.

The people were watching with rapt attention as he stood with his hands raised. There was a young woman directly in front of him with a crumpled five-dollar bill in her hand.

"Watch closely," the man announced, an Irish lilt in his voice.

He brought his hands on either side of the crumpled bill, but with at least six inches of space between them. With a small wave of his hand, the bill lifted off and rose slowly into the air.

The woman, her mouth open, stepped back, and now the bill floated in mid-air. As the red-haired performer made gestures, the bill remained in one place, unmoving in its spot and apparently unaffected by gravity.

Then, with a wiggle of his fingers, the money rose into the air toward his right hand and hovered a few inches below his fingers. Then it lowered down to his knees, and he brought his thumbs and middle fingers together, joined to form a loop over the floating note.

As a finale, the bill rose quickly into the air again and looked as if it might fly away completely. With a small jump, the man reached up and plucked the bill from the air, and offered it to the lady as the crowd applauded.

The woman, with a smile, examined the note and found it to be just a five-dollar bill. With a laugh, she dropped it into a small bucket in front of the man. People in the crowd threw bills into the tin.

"We gotta break this up, folks," Terrell announced and the crowd groaned in annoyance.

But the young man still wore the microphone and he spoke up. "Now folks, don't be mad at the officers, they're just doing their job. But, if you liked the show, give what you can!"

The man stepped off the bench, and his hand slid to a switch on the headset. "Sorry, officers, a lady asked me to show her a trick, and I didn't know it would end up as a show."

Terrell watched the crowd as they dispersed. Pro approached the young man. "You're pretty good. But you know you can't do that here."

As they spoke, people continued to drop bills and pocket change into the bucket on the ground.

"I'm terribly sorry, officer," he said with an accent that Pro thought was one of the sexiest things she ever heard. He took off the hat in a gesture of respect. "I normally work the parks. But I just came from an audition, and I had me equipment. This little girl recognized me, so I did a trick. Suddenly, I had a crowd, and I figured, why not?"

"Well, mister—"

"Tobin, Jamie Tobin. I go by Tobin the Great," he added modestly.

Terrell stepped up at this point as the crowd had moved on. "You know, we could give you a citation for blocking the sidewalk."

"I understand, officer. It shan't happen again." The man picked up the bucket and dumped its contents into a medium-sized leather bag and followed it with the microphone and the speaker off his belt.

"Do you have a license to street-perform?" Terrell continued, not yet mollified.

"A license?" the man queried. "Is that something you need?"

"This is New York City, buddy. You need a license," Terrell insisted.

"Wait, Officer Hodges," Pro said, slipping into the formal use of his name. "If he sticks to the parks, I think we can let him go."

Terrell gave Jamie a dirty look.

Pro continued, "But, if so, can you do a favor for us?"

Jamie smiled, all Irish charm. "For you, darlin', I'll do anything you ask."

"Easy, buddy," Terrell growled. "That's my partner."

"Are you familiar with any other buskers?" Pro went on.

This made Jamie's eyebrows rise in surprise that she knew the term. "Buskers, eh? I met quite a few since I got here, ma'am."

The Irishman's more respectful tone towards Pro calmed Terrell.

"Do you know a magician named Mick Wexler?"

There was a flash of anger in Jamie's eyes, but he quickly covered it with his charming smile. "Mickey? Why, sure. We've met a few times, shared a couple of corners."

"Could I meet with you?" Pro suggested. "I'd like to know everything you can tell me about him."

This got a lifted eyebrow and a dirty look from her partner that she ignored.

Jamie grew suspicious. "Why…what's he done?"

Terrell intoned darkly. "He ain't done nothing. He's dead."

Jamie's color changed, as his eyes shifted back and forth to Terrell and Pro. "Dead?" He said in a shocked voice. "How?"

Pro's jaw set and she gave Terrell a look that he ignored. "Murdered."

Jamie considered this for a moment. "You don't think I—"

"Nothing like that," Pro assured. "But I would be interested in your insights. Let me know who were his friends or anything that could help."

Jamie nodded, and Pro could tell this saddened him. "Aye, I can do that if it would help."

Pro took out her notebook, and Jamie quickly jotted down his cell number. He also wrote a quick note under it, then he gave Pro a smile as he returned the notebook.

He put his hat back on. "Well, I'm off then. Thank you for your understandin', officers." He gave a wave and hastened away.

"Block no more sidewalks," Terrell yelled after him.

"You didn't have to be so tough on him," Pro said, as they turned and headed for the car.

"Watch out for that guy. He's slick," Terrell warned. "All that damn Irish charm."

Pro glanced at her notebook. The cell number was there, a standard 10 digit one, that suggested the Irishman had gotten the phone here in the states. But under the number he had written:

Call me. Without your partner, please.

This made Pro smile as she got back into the car. He had indeed been charming, and she felt a slight attraction to the green-eyed man.

Then she wondered when she had noticed his green eyes.

2. The Promise

S he sat and waited in a little place on First Avenue near 8th Street. It was a hole-in-the-wall with wrought-iron chandeliers decorated with fake candles and small electric bulbs for the lighting. The bar was dark wood, as were the walls, and it had the feel of an old speakeasy pulled out of another time. Behind the bar was a tall man with brown hair that was swept to one side of his head. He wore a simple formal shirt, black pants, and a black bowtie and an apron.

Pro had a glass of white wine in front of her, and she glanced at the door to see Jamie saunter in.

He had changed into a black shirt and black pants, and he still wore a vest, this time a simple black one with a pattern in the fabric. Hatless, and it was plain that he'd actually brushed his hair, which instead of a fiery mop, was now contoured to compliment his face. He held a large coin in his hand, and now and then, he would manipulate it so that it walked over his fingers.

"You clean up well," Pro praised, as he drew near, and he gave a quick turn to show off his entire ensemble.

He gave Pro the once over. She was wearing black pants and a white blouse with a short jacket on over it. "You clean up well, too, officer. Thanks for calling and asking to meet me. Sorry, I'm late." He took the barstool next to her.

"I was getting worried," she chided.

"Oh, Miss Pro, any man who'd stand you up would be a fool," Jamie prattled. He gave a nod to the bartender, who returned it. "Guinness, please."

"I was afraid you were going to go for the whiskey."

"No, Ma'am. Not when you work the hours I do," he explained as the coin again traveled over his knuckles. "Or the work I do."

"From my knowledge of magicians, you only work on weekends."

"Not a busker who wants to have a little extra cash. I go down to Wall Street during lunch, and I perform after school in the park, sunny days. I like to have a bit of comfort in me work."

The bartender placed a glass of dark brown beer in front of Jamie and he took a healthy sip. "Ah, that's good."

Pro pulled out her notebook. "So I wanted to ask you—"

"Miss Pro, can we have a moment to relax before the questions? Have ye eaten?"

"Eaten? Um... no... but I—"

"Well, the least I can do is buy you a meal for not takin' me away in irons, as your partner seemed to want to do."

"Terrell is very protective of me."

His face grew serious, and he lowered his voice. "You're not...y'know...involved with him, are ye?"

Pro flushed. "Nothing like that. He's been married forever. He just feels he needs to watch out for me."

This made him smile. "That's good. In your line of work, you need someone like that. Someone who's got yer back."

"And I can buy my own dinner," she insisted.

"Tell you what, the portions here are huge. We'll split some fish and chips. Do you like it with malt vinegar?"

"Doesn't everyone?" Pro laughed.

The pair moved to a small round table. There was a square plastic holder with salt, pepper, mustard in a jar, a squeeze bottle of ketchup, and paper napkins. At the two place settings were a fork, butter knife, and a spoon.

Jamie took the padded seat, which was a long bench with a vinyl back and a large cushion that was the second seat for four tables that were in a row.

Pro gingerly took the single chair that faced him.

This almost feels like a date, ran through her mind, and she felt herself get a little warm. *How long has it been since I've been on an actual date?*

A bored waitress, a tall young woman with hair that was two colors, dark black and blond, was staring at her smartphone in a corner. She wore a dress that had blue and white with stripes and had a tiny apron that was more decorative than functional. Slipping her phone into her pocket, she approached, and with a totally uninterested glance, asked, "Whaddya want?"

Jamie gave her his dazzling smile. That got her attention. "One order of Fish and Chips, darlin'."

She returned his smile despite herself, ignored Pro, and walked away.

"So, Jamie, is that short for James?"

"Just call me Jamie," he told her with dimples appearing on his face.

Pro tried to focus on business. "Okay," she stated and pulled out her notebook a second time. "How do you know Mick Wexler?"

"I met him shortly after I got here. I'm on a Tourist Visa, and I've been in the states about five months."

"I thought with a Tourist Visa, you couldn't work."

"Who's working?" he shrugged. "I just show some people a few tricks and they choose to give me money!"

"Tax-free money!"

"I like to think of it as a donation to a worthy cause," Jamie leaned close and said, "You're not with the IRS as well, are ye?"

"No, just NYPD, but I should frown on what you are doing."

"I'm not hurting anyone, and I'm spreading glee wherever I go." The coin flipped over his fingers again. "Let me show you a trick."

"Hold it," Pro told him, pointing her pen like a weapon. "I don't need to see anything. I'm really not interested in magic."

"That's because you haven't seen a good magician!" As he spoke, he held the large coin out at the tips of his left fingers. He grabbed it with his right hand and then blew on the fingers and opened the hand to show that the coin was gone.

Pro sighed. "Not a bad French Drop, but I've seen better."

Jamie's eyes grew wide. "So, you *know* magic, then?"

Pro lowered her head. "I really didn't want to go into this. I want to talk to you about Mick Wexler."

"Oh come now, it's a big turn-on when a woman actually knows the name of a move and can recognize it."

"Well, not to me," Pro said, and folded her arms.

"Okay, but there must be an explanation. Did you learn magic as a child? Did you want to do it before you became a cop?"

Pro blew out a frustrated breath and looked down at the table. "No. My bio-dad is a magician."

"Your bio-dad?" he repeated, unsure.

"He was…is…a magician in Vegas. He walked out on my mom and me when I was six."

Jamie leaned back in the chair and observed her sagely. "I can see why that might put you off magic."

"Yeah. I used to go to shows with him all the time when I was little. And he used to take me out to places like this," Pro suddenly appeared quite angry. "And here I am, out with a damn magician."

"Miss Pro, I'm sorry—"

"I don't need your pity. This was a stupid idea. I'm going to leave."

She reached for her purse, just as the dispassionate waitress plopped a plate of fried fish with large steak fries onto the table between them.

"Now, Pro, this is far too much for me," Jamie said gently, not reaching for her or doing anything but sitting there. "Please, share a meal, ask me your questions. I won't do any more tricks."

Pro looked at him with suspicion.

He drew an imaginary 'X' over his heart. "Cross me heart."

Pro adjusted herself in the seat and looked at the food. "You're right, the portions are big," she murmured sullenly.

"It's why I come here. Makes an inexpensive date for a traveling man."

"This is *not* a date," Pro snapped, her eyes still on the food.

Jamie held up his hands. "All right, makes an inexpensive interrogation, then."

The waitress came out and plopped a bottle of malt vinegar on the table with all the aplomb of an annoyed teenager. Pro grabbed it, unscrewed the cap, and doused the plate with it liberally. Pro also grabbed the convenient squeeze bottle of ketchup and held it out to a suspicious glare from Jamie.

"For the fries," Pro explained.

"Only on your half, Miss Pro. I'm a purist."

This made Pro laugh despite herself. She put the red sauce in a small mound on the only empty corner of the large plate. She then speared a fry with her fork, dipped in the sauce and shoved it in her mouth.

The fry was delicious, warm and toasty. The ketchup was the perfect complement, and the slightly bitter tang of the vinegar made it a totally wonderful experience. She closed her eyes in pleasure.

"Wow, you really like chips," Jamie noted.

"I eat in a hurry, and usually cold sandwiches," Pro explained. "This is nice." She stabbed a second fry.

Jamie cut into the golden-brown shell of the cooked fish, exposing the white flesh underneath. He took a forkful and ate it.

"So, what do you want to know about Mickey?"

"Do you know if anyone was threatening him?"

Jamie shook his head and took another forkful of fish. "Probably everyone who ever met him."

Pro stopped chewing. "Come again?"

"Mickie was a nasty fellow, no disrespect to the dead. He made a point of annoying other performers and trying to prove he was better and smarter than they are. To be honest, I'm surprised he lasted this long."

"So you're not a fan?"

"Well, when I first got here to the states, Mickey put me up at his place a couple nights. But I soon learned he was not the sort I wanted to be associated with."

"Why is that?"

"He was always arguing with other performers, berating them as it were. Plus, he had a habit of getting involved in 'inappropriate' relationships."

"Inappropriate in what way?"

"He was always trying to steal other people's women," Jamie explained. "I don't know what it was, a competition to him or something. But if he saw a magician or performer with a pretty girl, he'd do his best to woo her away."

This made Pro laugh. "Woo her?"

"Hey, I'm Irish. That's how we speak."

She covered her mouth and controlled herself. "Sorry. Is there anything you can tell me from when you stayed at his place?"

Jamie considered this. "He was very security conscious. He'd put a paper match in his door."

"A paper match." Pro frowned. "Why?"

"Oh, Miss Pro, you've neglected watching old detective movies. You do that to see if anyone opened your door while you were away."

Pro nodded. "I see. If the match is on the floor, someone came into your room."

"Good! But, more'n that, if the match is missing, that's a sign, too. And since it was a paper match, most people won't notice if it falls to the floor."

Pro scribbled in her notebook as she speared a piece of the white fish as well. "Anything else?"

Jamie glanced up at the ceiling in thought. "When I first got here, we shared a spot—"

"Shared a spot?" Pro repeated, unsure of the term.

"We'd work a location together, you know, to have a mate watch yer back."

"Ah, yes. You would find a place in the park and then take turns?"

"Exactly. Made things more fun. I'd do a show, then Mickey would. The other fellow kept an eye on the tip—do you know what that is?"

"The tip is Carny lingo for the crowd," Pro sneered.

"Buskers use a lot of carny lingo. You certainly are knowledgeable," Jamie marveled. "But the thing is, whenever we set up, he'd always look around first like he was checking for someone."

"Really?" Pro observed and wrote in the notebook, then impaled another fry.

"One time he looked around, then stopped and insisted we go to a location at the far end of the park. Another time, he looked around, froze, then turned to me and said he'd forgotten an appointment."

"Suspicious, I suppose," Pro commented. "But not outside of the realm of possibility. Did you see anyone lurking about?"

"Lurking? Can't say I did. But, to give the devil his due, Mickey was a good performer. When we shared a spot, we did well for both of us. He taught me that in New York, keep your show to ten or fifteen minutes. People are in a hurry, even in the park."

Another glass of white wine and Guinness was plunked down in front of them by the surly waitress.

Pro looked at the glass and noticed that her first one had only a sip left. "I didn't order this."

"No, I did," Jamie countered. "My treat."

She gave him a suspicious look, then relented and poured the last mouthful from the old glass into the new one.

Jamie smiled as she did this. "So why are you looking into his murder? I thought that was a detective's job."

Pro shrugged. "I want to be a detective. If I can help solve the case, it will help get me there."

"Won't the detectives resent you taking it upon yourself?"

"I'll share anything I learn with them and try not to get in their way."

"Well, I always try to avoid the police. Present company excluded," he added as he took a sip of the beer.

They continued to eat, and Pro had to admit, Jamie was a charmer. He told her about his family in Ireland, and his desire to be a magician in the United Kingdom. "That's why I come to the states, y'see. A lot of chances to perform, and some of the best magicians in the world are giving lectures."

"You go to lectures?"

"Sure, there is a magic club here, called *Magic Over Manhattan*. There's a meeting every month on a Thursday, and for ten dollars you get to see lectures by some of the best out there."

"How did you find out about that?"

He shrugged. "Mickey took me there, introduced me around. That's before I found out everyone hated him."

"Is there anything else you can think of? I mean, is there anyone who might benefit from Mickey being dead?"

Jamie munched on a fry and considered it. "A lot of the guys at *Magic Over Manhattan*. You wouldn't believe all the people who claimed Mickey took advantage of him: Jack Gallagher, Todd Dagger—"

"Wait! A guy's name is Dagger?"

"It's not his real name. He's a knife-thrower."

"A knife-thrower?" Pro repeated.

"Aye, he uses his lady as a target. Throws knives around her in his show."

Pro shuddered involuntarily. "How…nice…"

"There's this one fellow, but he—oh never mind…"

"Please, any lead might help."

"At the magic club, this one fellow calls himself Diablo."

"Diablo? Like 'the devil?'"

"Aye. He and Mickey did not like each other, and the fellow tried to embarrass Mick anytime he could."

"Do you think he could have wanted to hurt Mickey?"

"Well, at the last meeting, he threatened to kill him."

3. The Turn

A fter the meal was finished, she had made plans with Jamie to attend the magic club meeting, which was the next evening. Jamie insisted on walking Pro to catch her subway. On one hand, Pro felt she could handle herself, but it was a gesture that was sweet if unnecessary.

After all, Pro was the one who carried a gun.

On the ride out to Brooklyn, it amazed Pro that her mind kept going back to Jamie, his bright eyes and his relaxed smile. She had told herself he wasn't her type.

Her last relationship had been while she was going to the Police Academy with Julius Trent, who was now assigned to the 125th Precinct. He was definitely her type, a tall African-American man with a shaved head and the body of a weight-lifter. They had had a friendly competition during training to push themselves to excel. This also led to nights of some very satisfying sex.

Upon reflection, Pro realized it had been over a year since she'd taken a lover, or been taken by one. The demands of the job left her too tired most days to even think about dating. Added to that, the concepts of cyber-dating or any of the online sites with available men for an intimate encounter did not appeal to her.

In fact, she found some of these sites downright creepy.

But Jamie, with his warm smile and his courtly manners, had a certain rough charm. The problem was, he knew exactly how charming he was, and it was probably what made him a good magician.

All these thoughts and unbidden feelings coursed through her mind and made her body shiver. The subway car reached her stop, and she walked out of the station toward her small studio apartment.

Her apartment was basically one room, and not a large one at that, though it had a large closet. Two even tinier rooms branched off from the main: one alcove was a kitchenette—you wouldn't dare call something that small an actual 'kitchen.' The only other room was the bathroom with a shower stall.

She unloaded her police sidearm and put it in her lockbox that was stored in the closet, pulled the folding bed out of the sofa, undressed and got in bed.

She was tired from another physical day on the job, which was good. But the vision of Jamie Tobin still danced in her brain, and she wondered what he'd look like undressed.

As naked images of Jamie coursed through her mind, she slipped off to sleep.

In their police car the next day, Pro was observing the neighborhood as she and Terrell drove down 54th Street, cruising the area.

"You want to tell me about it?" Terrell asked.

Pro jumped back to reality. "I'm sorry, tell you about what?"

"What's on your mind? You've been distant all day, not talking except to say 'yes' or 'no,' and you keep looking out the window and sighing."

Pro started. Had she been sighing? Out loud?

"I'm just thinking about the Wexler murder."

Terrell frowned as he drove. "That's homicide's problem now, not ours."

"I know, but I did some follow-up last night."

"Follow-up?"

"Yes, I had a chat with Jamie Tobin."

"That Irish guy we should've busted yesterday, but you got all soft and wobbly?"

Pro felt her back stiffen. "I did not get soft and wobbly," she snapped. "You take that back!"

"Alright, alright. You met him after work?"

"Yes. There's a magic society or club or something, and they have a meeting tonight. According to Jamie, there was someone in this club who threatened Wexler. The guy calls himself 'Diablo.'"

"The devil?" Terrell considered this as he turned onto Seventh Avenue. "Well, that's good."

Now it was Pro's turn to frown. "Aren't you going to tell me to leave it to the detectives or that we're busy enough?"

"Nope," he replied simply. "I'm just glad to hear you're going out."

"I thought you didn't like Jamie."

Terrell chuckled. "I don't, but if he gets your sorry rear end out of your little apartment and shows you a good time, that's all right in my book."

A call came over their radio, and the pair were off to focus on nothing more daunting than a simple traffic accident.

As soon as the shift was over, Pro called her mother. When Pro asked if Elisha might have a dress that would impress, it pleased the older woman. Pro had budget-friendly clothing, while Elisha had more sophisticated and fashionable attire.

It helps to have a mom the same dress size as you.

Pro had ridden the subway up to 86th Street and walked the block over to West End Avenue, waved at the doorman, who knew her from weekly visits. She rode the elevator up and knocked on her mother's door.

Elisha greeted her with a hug.

"So, you want to look nice tonight. Is it for a date?" Elisha asked with hope, wanting to know the details.

"Actually, it's for a magician's club. I want to impress."

Elisha stopped dead and turned slowly toward her daughter. "You want to impress…magicians?" Her voice carried a tone of disbelief. "I mean…after your father…"

"Please Momma, I don't want to talk about Max."

"But baby, he *is* your father—"

"No. Joe was my father, and he's gone," Pro stated firmly.

"I know," Elisha sighed. "Believe me, I know it every night."

Pro gazed at the floor, embarrassed. "I'm sorry Momma, of course, it's harder on you than on me."

"It's facing that empty bed that's the hardest for me. I'm finally beginning to get to sleep without taking something."

"You've been taking pills to help you sleep?" Pro worried.

Elisha waved her hand at her daughter in a dismissive gesture. "Just an over-the-counter thing. And not every night. But sometimes, this place is awful quiet."

"Only a New Yorker could say that," Pro mused. "Between sirens, traffic, and everything else, this place is never *really* quiet."

"It has been lately," Elisha responded sadly. Then her eyes lit up. "Now let's find you a dress."

Pro quickly brought Elisha up to speed on the case, and her plan to see if she could get information from the meeting of *Magic Over Manhattan*. Meanwhile, Elisha pulled dresses, held them up to her taller daughter and rejected certain choices.

"I think if I show a little leg, it will distract the magicians, get them to drop their defenses," Pro opined.

Elisha huffed. "You could go topless and *really* distract them. But no daughter of mine is going out like that."

"Yes, Mother," Pro mocked.

"So what about this boy you're going there with?"

"Well, I have to say, he's not really a boy, he's a man."

Elisha lifted an eyebrow. "Oh, really?"

"Don't get any ideas. He's not my type at all. He's a skinny Irish guy with a lot of charm."

"You never know," Elisha told her with a knowing look. "Some skinny white guys are pretty surprising. And magicians are very good with their hands."

"Momma!" Pro replied in shock.

"Just sayin'." Elisha chuckled. "I know you haven't been on a date in the longest time."

"The job takes all my energy. Besides, this isn't a date, it's an investigation."

"Won't the detectives mind if they find out that you're looking into this?"

Pro shrugged. "I'll tell them anything I find. Right now, there isn't much to tell."

By this time, the two women had agreed on a dress, and although it was shorter on Pro than it would be on her mother, it didn't show too much leg.

Pro spent a half-hour on her makeup, and she had left a pair of heels at Elisha's apartment. This made sense, since the only time she got dressed up it was usually in one of her mother's outfits.

"Okay if I crash here tonight?" Pro asked.

"You know where your room is. Just come in quietly." Then her mother gave her a wicked look. "Unless you end up at *his* place."

"Not happening," Pro told her as she threw on a wrap and headed out the door.

However, on the subway ride to the village, she thought about it. What if Jamie made a pass? How should she handle it? Politely decline? Vehemently refuse?

She sighed and focused on her small notebook, which was in her purse with her service weapon, handcuffs, and her officers' badge backer from her uniform. This held her badge, name tag, and citation ribbons. It would come in handy if the situation pressed her into an arrest.

She doubted it would, but it was better to be prepared.

Once she got off the subway, she walked towards Washington Square Park. She noted with the eye of a cop that she was getting a lot of stares from the men she passed. She tried to relax and enjoy it. It had been a long time since she dressed up, and she had to admit she liked the attention. It made her feel attractive and desirable.

She strode up the street and approached the Washington Square Arch. This was a multi-storied construction built to celebrate the centennial of George Washington's inauguration.

It was the perfect downtown meeting place. Built in the style of the *Arc de Triomphe* in Paris, it was very large, made of white marble, and lit dramatically with multiple spotlights.

As Pro stood and gazed up Fifth Avenue, a man smoking some aromatic herb approached her. He was a very skinny white guy with dark hair, a thin mustache, an unshaven chin, and a heavy denim coat.

"Hey baby, you lookin' for a good time?" he inquired through bad teeth.

With a tight expression on her face, Pro flashed the badge holder from her purse.

The man's eyes grew wide. "Uh... just askin'."

He hastily walked away.

Pro smiled. That had been satisfying.

"Well now, don't you look nice," Jamie praised.

Pro turned to see him approach through the park. He was wearing his black ensemble again, black shirt, black pants, and black patterned vest.

Pro was in a black dress that had exaggerated shoulders and left her arms bare, but her wrap covered them. She wore heels, which put her five-foot-eleven frame up to an amazing six-foot-two. This made her almost four inches taller than Jamie, who didn't seem thrown by a tall woman, but offered his arm, and Pro took it.

One point for him, thought Pro, pleased that her added height hadn't intimidated the Irishman.

It was only a few blocks to Lafayette Street, and using a doorway next to a small *bodega*, they went upstairs to a room that held about twenty people, mostly men.

There were voices prattling as they reached the top stair, but as soon as Pro walked through the door, silence fell over the room. She overdressed for the situation, as most of the young men wore jeans and t-shirts. Two older men wore mismatched suit jackets and casual pants, but everyone stared at Pro with awe.

"Why are they staring?" Pro whispered.

"I showed up with a girl," Jamie explained, and then he spoke up. "Evening everyone! We're not late, are we?"

One of the older gentlemen came forward, a thin man in a cheap jacket, with horn-rimmed glasses and white hair that stuck out in all directions.

Pro immediately recognized the man, though he was older than the times she had seen him selling things in his small magic shop.

He drew close to the newcomers. "Jamie, we're having a lecture tonight. We can't have any non-magicians here."

"It's all right Mister Floss, I'm sworn to secrecy," Pro announced.

Taken aback for a moment, the man's eyes grew small as he stared at Pro. "How do you know my name?"

Pro smiled. "Mister Floss, I was in your shop all the time as a kid. Don't you remember?"

The man's brows knitted. "No."

"I was usually with Max?"

He still didn't seem to get it.

"Max Marvell?" Pro attempted.

He stared at Pro's blue eyes, and a flash of recognition occurred. "My stars! Prophecy Martin!"

Another older man came over. He was shorter and stout, and he gazed at Pro in complete amazement. Then he spoke, "Little Prophecy?"

Pro turned her attention to the other man. "Hi, Mister Tanner. How are things going at your store?"

The stout man chuckled and took Pro's hand to shake it vigorously. "My goodness, little Prophecy Martin, but...gosh...not so little anymore. How is your father?"

The other people in the room went back to their business, which appeared to be showing each other card tricks.

"He's good," Pro assured as the background conversations in the room started up again. "I haven't seen him for a while..."

"That's understandable. Being in Vegas and all," Louis Tanner said and let go of Pro's hand. "I don't mean to stare, but you are even more beautiful than your mother."

"You knew my mom?" Pro frowned. This was a piece of history that Pro hadn't heard.

"Of course," Al Floss interrupted. "When your parents were dating, he brought her to all the stores. Often."

Tanner agreed. "I think it was just to make the rest of us green with envy. She was quite the beauty. How is she?"

"Still a beauty," Pro revealed. "I got this dress from her."

Al frowned at Jamie but spoke to Pro. "And what are you doing with this troublemaker?"

"Now, that's not fair, Mister Floss," Jamie protested.

"He's my date," Pro declared, much to Jamie's surprise. "I wanted to get back into the community a bit, and Jamie offered to bring me to the meeting."

Louis Tanner moved closer. "We're delighted to have you both. We'll be starting in a few moments."

The two men moved away. Floss still glared daggers at Jamie. The Irishman drew close to Pro. "Your date? Miss Pro, you are sending me mixed signals."

"Think of it as your 'cover,'" Pro jibed.

"Great, now I'm a spy," he smirked.

"So why was Floss so upset with you?"

"Something that happened at last month's meeting. I did me linking rings, and Al thought I stole a move of his."

"Wait, he was upset about a move?" Pro frowned. "Did you do his routine?"

"Not at all. The move was a silent spin link. Al says I stole it from him, but I came up with it years ago back in Ireland."

"So, both of you taught yourselves the same move?"

"That's my guess. I mean, I never saw him do it. Besides, it's the blinkin' Chinese rings. Everybody learned other people's moves."

Pro sighed. "I'd forgotten that magicians are so possessive."

"Not to say anything bad, because I *am* your date," Jamie divulged, "but word is that your father is one of the toughest on people who steal his routines."

Pro's eyes went cold. "You don't have to be careful. I haven't spoken to the man in over a decade."

"Just so you know."

Pro scanned the room. She noted she wasn't the only woman. Over in one spot in the room, there was a striking lady who was almost as tall as her. Her skin was a light tan color, suggesting Spanish ancestry, which was reinforced by her mass of dark hair and eyes so deeply brown they were almost black.

She stood next to a man a few inches shorter than her, who appeared to be Italian with a robust frame and dark hair, as well as a rather impressive mustache.

He stayed close to the woman, who seemed annoyed and avoided his attentions.

"Who's the woman over there?" Pro asked.

Since Pro was the only other woman, Jamie had no trouble spotting the raven-haired beauty. "That's Camila. The guy next to her is the knife-thrower I told you about."

Pro nodded. "Right, Todd Dagger. I thought he'd be taller."

"So did he, considering the way he acts," Jamie confided. "I'm surprised that Camila is with him. I heard they'd broken up."

"Where'd you hear that?"

He shrugged. "Around."

"So, who is 'Diablo?'"

"He's the one wearing black," Jamie said without pointing.

She scanned the room again nonchalantly. "Very funny, they're all wearing black."

"In the corner, with the pierced ears and chains across his chest."

Surreptitiously, Pro moved her eyes until she located the man in the corner, as promised. He was a big, well-muscled white man with a long Van Dyke beard and a shaved head. He wore numerous piercings in his ears, as well as metal in his nose and eyebrow. A pair of heavy chromed chains crisscrossed the front of his black t-shirt.

He stood out from the group because of his muscular physique. A lot of them were rather pasty, and some were overweight. But there was also a young man of Asian descent who was maybe sixteen, and a tall African-American man who wore thick glasses.

Al Floss spoke loudly to get everyone's attention. For an older man, he had a powerful voice. "Hey there, I want to ask everyone to move into the lecture room."

Jamie offered his arm and Pro took it, which gave her a chance to lean close and whisper. "So what happened between Mickey and Diablo?"

"Diablo said Mick was working his spot."

"Say what?" Pro murmured.

"Yeah, Diablo went into this whole thing about his spot has always been his spot, and people expect him to be there."

"Crazy reason to kill someone."

"Yeah," Jamie whispered. "We'll talk about it after."

They stepped through the open door to a slightly larger room. They set it up with folding chairs in rows around a platform at the far end. There was an aisle down the middle that allowed easy access to the stage. They had set up a large card table with a red tablecloth and a black velvet mat on it.

Mr. Tanner was in the room's front where a man stood next to him. He was tall and lithe, and though he was older, he moved like he'd spent his life as a dancer. He had small eyes, and his face had many lines, but they all seemed to come from smiling.

Jamie nudged Pro. "That's Harry Fitch, one of the great coin manipulators."

"Really?" Pro marveled. "He stayed at my parent's apartment once when he and my father were working on a show."

Jamie turned to her, amazed. "You keep surprising me, Miss Pro."

"And you're very talkative, Sh!" She put her finger in front of her mouth to tell him to be quiet.

He grinned, and his eyes returned to the stage.

Fitch turned to sit at the table, and he pulled out several large coins.

Tanner cleared his throat. "Gentleman, and—quite to our surprise—ladies. Tonight's lecturer is none other than Harry Fitch, who is going to share some of his amazing coin work with us."

The crowd applauded as Pro took in the room, noting there were about twenty people. She quickly eliminated people who lacked the sufficient strength to shove the knife deep into the chest of Mick Wexler. The man known as 'Diablo' certainly had the muscle mass, but there were several others as well who were not as big, but appeared strong.

Fitch picked up the stack of four coins, and with a quick move, he suddenly spread the coins between his fingers in an impressive coin fan flourish.

He then placed them on the table. "Thank you. It's a pleasure to be here at the monthly meeting of *Magic Over Manhattan*. I want to show some effects and break them down for you."

He placed the four coins on the corners of the black velvet mat in front of him on the table. Covering two of the coins with his hands, instantly one coin was gone, and as he lifted his other hand, the two coins were under it. He then covered the pair of coins with the opposite hand, then crossed his arms to cover the coin at a third corner, whereupon it promptly disappeared. He removed his hand to show that the pair were now a trio of shiny metal dollars.

For a finale, he covered the three and the solo remaining coin, and instantly all four coins were together and the single one had vanished.

"Now, let me break it down for you—" he began.

Just then, the door to the room came open, and everyone turned to see two men in cheap suits. One was an Asian man, who held up a detective's gold shield and announced loudly, "NYPD! Sorry to interrupt, but we need to ask everyone some questions!"

The other was an older man who told the room, "Please have your identification ready."

Pro muttered, "Crap" as she recognized Detective Chu and Detective Franks.

Under the control of the two detectives, they soon put all the attendees back in the waiting room. They commandeered the stage area for questioning.

The two men went through the crowd and quickly took names until Chu reached Pro and stopped. He glared at her for a moment until recognition kicked in.

"Officer Thompson?" Chu murmured so only Pro could hear.

"Yes, detective, that's me," Pro responded.

Chu then glanced at Jamie. "And you are?"

"Jamie Tobin, sir," Jamie offered.

"He's with me," Pro explained. "Actually, I'm with him, he's how I got in here."

Chu turned and called out. "Franks, I have the first two I want to question."

"Got that partner," Franks answered.

With a nod of his head, Tom Chu gestured to the door of the theater. The three people went in, and Chu closed the door behind them. "Please sit down!"

Neither Jamie nor Pro thought it was a suggestion.

Once seated near the back of the room, with Jamie on the aisle, Chu went on, looking at Pro first. "Okay, Officer Thompson, you want to tell me what you're doing here?"

"Yes, detective," Pro said as her back straightened. "I'm following up on the murder of Mickey Wexler."

Chu did not look pleased. "No, officer. *I'm* following up on the murder of Mister Wexler. Who gave you clearance on this?"

Pro and Jamie exchanged a glance and Jamie raised his eyebrows as if to say, "Uh-oh."

Pro cleared her throat. "No one, sir, I'm doing it on my own. Mister Tobin here was an associate of the deceased."

Jamie gave his best friendly smile. "We worked together sometimes."

"I know. One reason I came here tonight was to talk to Mister Tobin. My concern for you, officer, is why didn't you tell anyone about him?"

"Sir?"

Chu fumed, "Franks and I have spent a day trying to locate your friend here. Turns out he has no regular address."

"My partner and I ran into him performing, sir. He mentioned he knew the deceased and could offer some limited information. Last night, he suggested coming to the meeting to help me track down a lead. If the lead had panned out, I was going to talk to you and your partner tomorrow."

Chu folded his arms and looked unconvinced.

Jamie chimed in. "That's what she told me she was going to do, sir."

"Uh-huh," Chu responded. "And what information was that?"

Jamie looked from Chu to Pro, and Pro gave him a nod. "Well, one of the other magicians calls himself Diablo, threatened to kill Mickey just last month, sir."

"Really?" Chu said. "Well, that's not what I heard on the street."

Pro stared in surprise. "What did you hear, detective?"

"That it was Mister Tobin here who threatened Wexler... and I have witnesses."

4. The Performance

"**W**hat?" Pro blurted and turned to stare at her escort in shock. "You never told me that!"

Jamie rose, but Chu put a hand on his shoulder and gently pushed him back into his seat.

"It's not what you think," Jamie stressed to Pro, then turned to look at Chu. "And not what you think either!"

Chu walked around to the aisle and faced them both. "So, enlighten me."

"We had an argument, nothing more."

Chu's eyebrows went up. "An argument? Do you always threaten to kill people when you argue with them?"

"Um…no," Jamie attempted.

"So what was this argument about?" Chu insisted.

"He thought I had taken his tip!" Jamie babbled.

"His what?"

"His crowd," Pro interjected.

Chu looked back and forth from Pro to the Irishman. "His crowd…?"

"For his street show," Pro clarified. "Both Mickey and Jamie are buskers."

"Buskers? What the hell is a busker?"

"That's a term for a street magician," Pro told him, trying very hard not to sound petulant.

Chu frowned. "You seem to know a lot about this."

Pro found her patience had run out. "I was investigating, detective."

Chu glared at Pro and she suddenly felt embarrassed that she had been so brazen to the detective who was only doing his job. While she was the one who had inserted herself into a murder probe.

Chu, however, said nothing in response but turned his attention back to Jamie. "So, what was the threat?"

Jamie sighed. "It was in front of a crowd, and I just packed up my stuff and left."

"And you made a threat—what was it?"

Jamie hesitated. "As I left, I told him that sometimes I wanted to kill him, that's all. It wasn't a threat!"

Pro glared at Jamie. "Why didn't you tell me that when I first talked to you?"

Jamie opened his arms. "I didn't think it was relevant!"

"I see," Chu ordered. "Stay in that seat and don't move."

He gave a nod of his head to Pro and the pair moved to the corner of the room furthest from the young man, as Pro fumed.

"So, you seeing this guy?" Chu said, his eyes on Jamie.

Pro shook her head, her mouth a tight line. "No, I needed someone who could get me in. If I had known he was lying to me…"

"Well, I want him uptown and in interrogation. But I also need to get names and information here."

Pro considered it. "I could cuff him and get him up to the precinct."

Chu eyed her with suspicion. "You have cuffs?"

"In my purse with my service weapon," Pro grumbled and gave a sharp look at Jamie. "Probably show him some police brutality along the way."

Chu smiled despite himself. "I like your style, officer. But that won't be necessary. There is a car from the Seventh Precinct downstairs. They can transport the suspect."

"I'll go with him if you want me to, sir. I feel I owe you."

Chu conceded. "It would be a help. Why do you think you owe me?"

"I met someone who knew the deceased and didn't immediately pass his name to you. I should have."

Pro watched Chu visibly relax. "You didn't really do anything wrong, officer. But you need to know any information on a homicide is to be shared with the detectives on the case as soon as possible."

"It's a mistake I won't repeat, sir," Pro assured. "Any luck with the cell phone?"

It surprised Chu that she'd changed the conversation, but he quickly caught on. "You were right. It wasn't in the apartment. We had to track it down. We're still waiting for the data from the carrier." He then looked over at Jamie and said. "Please escort the prisoner to interrogation, officer."

"Yes, sir," Pro said with a hasty salute that got a snicker from Chu that made her flush red. She walked over to Jamie. "Stand up, please."

He rose, intimidated by Pro's tone.

"Turn around, please."

"Now, Pro, you can't believe I—"

In one quick move, Pro used the leverage her height gave her to swing him around and bend him forward so his head banged the back of the metal folding chair.

"Ow!" Jamie gasped.

She pulled her handcuffs from her purse and fastened one on his left wrist. "When I say turn around..." She clicked the other cuff on his right wrist. "You turn your ass around."

"Yes, ma'am," Jamie croaked, lightheaded from the impact with the chair.

She pulled him roughly upright. A small welt was over his eye from the hit against the chair, but Jamie could see that Pro was too angry to be sympathetic.

She turned to Chu. "Detective, talk to that Diablo guy..."

"Oh, we will."

"And the knife-thrower, Todd Dagger."

Chu paused. "Why?"

Pro hesitated and wondered why she'd said that. "I'm not sure. Since it was a knife attack, it couldn't hurt."

"If you say so, officer," Chu answered with a shrug.

Pro grabbed the cuffs that bound Jamie and led him out of the theater. They passed through the outer lobby quickly, and the people who waited were surprised to see Jamie in cuffs, being led out by his date.

She turned to Franks. "Detective, I am escorting this suspect to the Midtown North Precinct, where I will hold him for interrogation, as per Detective Chu."

Franks looked on as surprised as anyone, but his eyes met Chu's as he stepped out of the theater and gave him a nod.

Franks cleared his throat and replied gruffly, "Understood, officer."

Pro then took Jamie quickly down the stairs and out to the street. In front of the building, a police sedan with the traditional white with blue lettering waited with two officers standing outside it.

Pro muttered to Jamie. "You move one step, and I'll rip your balls off."

"I believe you," Jamie confessed.

"Officers," Pro said as she rooted through her purse and pulled out her badge holder with her name tag. "I am Officer Thompson, and Detective Chu asked me to escort this suspect to Midtown North. He told me I could catch a ride with you."

The first man, a rather pasty Caucasian fellow, looked up at the taller Pro. "Uh, yes, officer. But I'm afraid you'll have to ride in back with the prisoner."

"No problem, officer, thank you."

"Why are you dressed like that, officer?" the second man wondered aloud. He was also pasty, middle-aged with a gut.

"Undercover," Pro stated.

The uniformed officer opened the rear door, and Pro held Jamie's head down and shoved him in, then followed behind him. The back seat smelled of stale body odor left by a recent inhabitant. There was a mesh steel cage and bulletproof glass that separated them from the front seat of the car.

The two officers got into the car and pulled away from the curb and onto Lafayette, heading uptown until it became Fourth Avenue, and they continued north.

"Pro, I didn't do anything," Jamie murmured to her.

"You lied to me." She fumed, not looking at him.

"I didn't lie. I just didn't think it was important. I mean, I told you that Mickey was a nasty guy. He fought with everyone."

Pro leaned close to him with a glance at the officers. "So what really happened? Why did you threaten him?"

"I-I—"

"Don't give me that 'stole your tip' crap."

"I-I—"

"Because I knew that was bullshit, and so did detective Chu. You wanna get outta this? You better start being straight with us."

"Okay, okay, but not here." He indicated the officers with a shake of his head.

Pro gave a look at the two men and then turned back to Jamie. "They're busy. Talk quietly, and tell me the truth, or I will kick your Irish ass up two flights of stairs and into that interrogation room."

"Sure, sure," Jamie hissed. "The truth is Mickey moved in on a girl I was seein'."

"A girl you were seeing?" Pro repeated. "Like, dating?"

Jamie exhaled in frustration. "It weren't nothing serious, we went out a couple of times. But, when Mickey saw I liked her, he moves in and next thing I know she's stayin' at his place."

"You're telling me that Mickey was a *playa*."

"A — what?" Jamie asked in confusion.

"Whatever. So he moves in on this girl and you threaten to kill him."

Jamie looked at the floor. "I was...pretty steamed. Truth is, I just moved on, let it go, and stopped hanging out with him. Honestly, Pro, I didn't kill him."

"He threatened Mickey at the last meeting. That was true! And there's a lot more than him who wanted a piece of Mickey. He was always getting involved with women he shouldn't have. Word is, a jealous husband put him in the hospital about a year ago."

"That doesn't help me or you, Jamie."

"Okay, okay," Jamie fretted and sat quietly for a moment while he thought. "There is one other thing."

"I'm listening."

"Mickey was working on a new act."

"A new act?" Pro dismissed. "Wow, that's cause for murder."

But Jamie went on. "It is if he stole the act from someone else. And believe me, Mickey was not above that."

The car pulled in front of the large granite building for the Eighteenth Precinct, and Pro waited patiently for one officer to let them out.

"You still gonna kick my ass up two flights of stairs?" Jamie whispered.

"I haven't decided yet," Pro affirmed, as the door opened and she stepped out.

Jamie slid out, and Pro took his arm. She turned to the pasty cop. "Thank you, officer."

"You're welcome," the man took another look at Pro's dress, gulped, and got into the passenger seat. The car quickly pulled away.

Two buildings stood next to each other on 54th Street. One was the original police building with arched doorways and pillars carved into the second story stone facade. But Pro pulled Jamie into the squat, rectangular building next door, built years earlier to accommodate the expanding force.

She led him up the stairs to the second floor and down a long hall. They reached a door marked INTERROGATION C, and she opened it and pushed the magician in.

It was a small, dirty room with a table and four chairs. She sat him at the table that faced a huge mirror. Then she opened the cuffs, brought them around in front of his body and fastened them to a chain that ran through the table and bolted to the floor.

"Is this really necessary, Pro?" Jamie asked.

"I believe we're going to go back to Officer Thompson."

Jamie sighed as Pro stopped at the door. She hung her head, debating if she should say what she wanted to say. Finally, she turned to look at him from the open doorway. "You want to know the worst part? I was really beginning to like you."

Jamie looked stricken. "Pro, I like you too."

"Then I guess you should have been up front with me," Pro chided, and a flash of anger shone in her eyes. "You magicians are all the same."

She went out and slammed the door behind her, leaving Jamie alone in the room.

Pro went to her locker in the basement and changed into her uniform. She wanted Chu and Franks to see her as a cop when they arrived, and not a girl playing dress-up.

As she changed, she found her mind wandered to Jamie. The hurt look on his face when she left him in the interrogation room. Obviously, she was a sucker. When he looked at her with that 'I'm sorry' hangdog expression, the only thing she wanted to do was to move to him and press her lips to his.

What was it about this guy that got her so worked up? A skinny white guy, and a magician to boot! Everything that was a turnoff to her.

Yet, those green eyes that had moved up and down her body when he arrived to meet her in the park. That cocky smile that promised so much.

She slammed the door of her locker; the sound reverberated in the empty room. She sat on the nearby bench to put on her police regulation shoes and bit her lip to force down the mix of emotions.

She felt in her heart that Jamie wasn't the killer. For one thing, he lacked the physical stature and just plain old muscle power that the knife would have required.

What she needed to do was focus on the case.

There was something at the crime scene she had noticed, but she couldn't quite figure out what it was.

Fully dressed, she went back to the interrogation room and watched Jamie through the one-way glass.

He looked very despondent and had laid his head down on the table. A part of her wanted to go to him, hold him, and tell him everything would be all right. Another part of her wanted to go in and scream at him, maybe smack his face on the table a few times for emphasis.

"Prisoner okay?" a voice said, and Pro started, which shook her out of her reverie.

Chu and Franks came in. Franks had a handcuffed and unspeaking Diablo by one arm. The big man looked sullen and uninterested in what was happening.

Pro found her voice. "Umm…yes sir, he's in 'C.'"

Chu gave her a nod. "Good. Franks, put our guest in 'B,' please."

"Got it."

Chu smiled and moved next to Pro to peek in the window.

"Sir, I have a request."

Chu looked over. "Yes, officer?"

"Would it be possible to look over the crime scene photos?"

Chu frowned. "The crime scene? Why?"

Pro floundered for a moment. "I'm not sure, sir."

"That's not very helpful, officer."

Franks came out of the interrogation room and moved closer to the pair as they spoke.

"I think I saw something at the scene. It might be the answer to this entire case."

Chu exhaled loudly. "I don't know, officer…"

Franks drew close. "Come on, Tom. What could it hurt? We have witnesses to interrogate, anyway."

Chu glared at his partner, then relented. "Okay, come with me."

Chu headed off and Franks whispered to Pro, "Good hunting, officer."

Pro gave him a smile as they entered the nearby detective's bullpen. It was a large open room, with pairs of desks all around. Since it was night, there wasn't anyone there, but Pro could imagine it in the busy daytime: people bustling, phones jangling, the smell of old coffee.

She immediately felt at home.

Chu went to his desk and pulled open a drawer. He grabbed a manila folder and placed it on the desk.

"I might need the photos of the DB for the interrogations," Chu explained.

"That's fine, sir. I only need the scene. Oh, and do you have any photos of the murder weapon?"

"They're in there," Chu said as he grabbed several eight-by-ten photos of the very dead Mickey Wexler.

"Thank you," Pro stated. "Also, detective, Mister Tobin related the vic ended up in the hospital about a year ago after an altercation with a jealous husband —"

"Already looked into that angle, officer, and cleared it. He was one of the first people we ran down and questioned."

"Yes, sir. But I only found out this information and wanted to make sure you knew."

Chu smiled. "Good. That's the way it should be, officer."

He walked out as Pro slowly went through the photographs taken at the scene. The forensic team had been very thorough, even taking shots of the magic props on the bookcases and in the bedroom. Pro was also pleased when she saw photos of the bedding, and that the blood had soaked in, just as she had theorized.

She reached the photos of the large sheet of plywood that Wexler had in the bedroom's corner. The technicians took photos of the framed piece of wood with the cloth covering it, then with the cloth removed. She looked at the pock-marked and dented wood, and tried to understand what could have caused the thin vertical marks. She wondered why were there no such marks in the center of the panel.

Nothing came to mind.

Why would a man, a street magician, have such a large piece of wood framed and stored in his bedroom? If it was a prototype for a magic trick, it didn't seem to have any useful application.

She continued through the photos, but that was the only one that pulled at her. Finally, she reached a photo of the knife used for the murder.

It was black with that strange circle of metal at the end of the pommel, and a long and wicked blade, with a hilt wrapped in some kind of black nylon cord. It gave the appearance of something a ninja might use. Pro thought back to the young Asian man she'd seen at the meeting, then immediately dismissed him. He didn't appear to have the upper body strength it would take to do the job.

She sat there and tried to decide what had triggered her concerns, but could not find the connection.

With a glance at her watch, she realized it was almost 10:00 PM. She was due back at the station in a little less than ten hours. With a sigh, she closed the folder and tried to see if a night's sleep might jog what she was trying to remember into place.

"Any luck, officer?" Chu asked.

She stood as Chu approached the desk. "I'm afraid not. But there is something. I just haven't figured it out yet." She pulled the photo of the plywood sheet. "What do you make of this, sir?"

He glanced at the photo. "Oh that. Yeah, Franks and I saw that."

"It's pretty unusual, sir. An eight-foot by four-foot sheet of heavy plywood framed with two-by-fours."

Chu shrugged. "Franks and I figured it was a practice stage. You know, put it out on the floor of the living room to practice his tricks."

"I don't think so, sir. See all the pockmarks? Why would a stage have all that damage just from practicing his act?"

"Well, let me know if you have any ideas," Chu added dismissively.

"Yes, sir," Pro sighed.

"We're letting your boyfriend go."

"He is *not* my boyfriend," Pro barked, surprised by the strength of her reply.

Chu grinned. "I know. I figured that out when you head-butted him against the chair."

Pro flushed a bit at this and mumbled, "The suspect wasn't cooperating."

Chu let loose with a boisterous laugh. "But you handled him quickly and efficiently, officer."

Pro smiled. "Well, he cooperated after that. How come you're letting him go?"

Chu shrugged. "His alibi checked out. He was at an event, doing close-up magic when the murder occurred."

"What was TOD, sir?" Pro asked, wanting to know the time of death.

"About ten o'clock at night, two days before you and Officer Hodges found him."

Pro considered this. "Okay, well, I am going to change, sir."

Chu nodded. "And by the way, officer, that dress…"

Pro turned.

"You looked good in it," Che said simply.

Pro's smile grew wider. "Thank you, detective."

"Any time, officer," he told her and returned to his desk with the folder of photos.

Pro headed down to the locker room and quickly changed back into the dress and heel. She returned her service weapon to her purse, but left her badge-holder and handcuffs.

As she walked out of the precinct, Jamie was there waiting.

"Pro, I needed to talk to you—"

She turned up her nose and walked down the street away from him. "I have nothing to say to you."

He ran to catch up to her. "Please, Pro, I really didn't think that threat was a big thing. It was weeks ago, and I'd forgotten it."

She gave him a quick glance that suggested he was a lower form of life. "Look, we're very different and I got a thing about men being straight with me."

He moved in front of her, "Please Pro, just hear me out."

Pro folded her arms. "Make it quick, and then get out of my way or I will move you."

"I don't doubt that," he attempted as a joke. Seeing that it failed, he became serious. "The truth is, I like you, Pro."

She pushed past him and stomped her way towards the subway. Not easy in heels. "Then you should've been straight with me."

"Can we start over? I promise I'll be totally honest."

She stopped and faced him. "No magic tricks?"

"None, unless I need your professional opinion."

She considered it. "Okay, that's fair."

"Can I call you then?"

"Let me think about it. If so, I'll call you," she replied and noticed they had reached the subway entrance.

"That's great," he said and leaned towards her.

She body-blocked him, her arms up and ready to fight. "What are you doing?"

He leaned back. "Sorry. I was trying to kiss you. I've wanted to do that since yesterday."

"So you just lean in, like you're all that?"

He grew puzzled. "All what?"

"Exactly!" Pro responded, which confused Jamie even more. "Let's be clear. If I want to be kissed, you'll know it."

"How will I?" he asked innocently.

"Because it will look like this," she answered. She grabbed him by the lapels of his vest and pulled him to her, fixing her lips to his in a heated kiss.

The feeling was like putting a live electric wire to her mouth. The electricity started at her feet and coursed through her, heating her body with a fire that she wanted to satisfy. Right here, right now.

She pushed him back, and the pair stared at each other in utter disbelief. Pro realized that, apparently, he'd felt it as well.

Without a thought, both of them moved to each other and renewed the kiss. This time opening their mouths so their tongues touched and played, and it filled Pro with a feverish need. She felt her hips move against his body and was aware that he was excited as well.

"Get a room," some middle-aged guy jeered as he walked down the stairs and into the subway.

With a gasp, Pro pulled back, suddenly aware of where they were and what they were doing. She was a cop. She couldn't be necking with a guy down the street from her precinct.

Jamie was panting and appeared as if someone had drugged him. "Oh my," was all he could manage.

"Yeah," Pro muttered and her hand when to her hair. She felt like she'd undergone an out-of-body experience. "I... uh... have to go. I'll... uh... call."

"Please do," Jamie told her, his eyes burning into her.

She pushed past him while she could still control herself and rushed down the stairs and onto the subway.

Everything had changed, and she didn't know what to do about it.

5. The Build

At her mother's apartment, Pro slept fitfully. The unexpected reaction to kissing Jamie had wound her body in a cocoon of desire. It had been a year since she had indulged in physical love, the feelings and wants pushed down as she focused on her job.

But now, her body had betrayed her iron will, pushing out the thoughts of duty and self-control. Replacing them were images of touching, tasting, and the joining of bodies in a dance that seemed part of an ancient past, but now aflame in her.

She finally put her pillow between her legs and drifted off into the realm of dreams. In sleep, strange visions combined with erotic memories. She was naked in bed with her former lover, Julius Trent. He touched and caressed her, then entered her body vigorously. All at once, Jamie replaced the big, black man and moaned and mumbled words of adoration as he moved inside her.

As the motions increased and sped up, the two men switched places repeatedly until she was unsure with whom she was making love. One moment it was Jamie, the next Julius, then it seemed her lover transformed into every man she'd ever taken to bed, which was only four.

A shuddering climax woke her, so strong that it forced her to sit up as she squeezed the pillow with her legs. She sat there, gasping, shivering, and fighting to catch her breath, as she cursed the annoying distraction.

After a few minutes, she calmed down and had to admit; she felt much more relaxed. She lay back down to sleep, finally at peace.

But towards morning, a very different dream coalesced. It was years earlier, and she was with her mother and father. Her real father.

Max Martin aka Max Marvell.

She looked up at him, the tall thin Caucasian man she adored, who was truly magical. He glanced down with a smile and Pro saw his bright blue eyes, the same color as her own. He was holding her hand, his skin so pale compared to her coffee-and-cream skin tone. Holding her other hand was her dark mother, and they were walking outside at a carnival.

It had been a rare Saturday outing, as that was the day her father usually worked. But he'd taken the time off to bring her to an old-fashioned carnival somewhere in New Jersey. There was a clear autumn sky, and the weather was warm. They set up games to play, and large rides on the back of trucks. They put the entire fair up in a field some place; she wasn't sure where.

Pro had been on the rides, eaten cotton candy, won a small stuffed bear, and they walked up to a set of bleachers near where a show was being presented.

It was the best day ever.

In front of her was a small raised wooden platform. And at the back of the platform were panels of wood standing on end, painted red. There was a large target painted in white circles.

There was something important about it, but Pro just couldn't understand what it was.

Why did it matter? She was there with her mommy and daddy, her momma was young and beautiful and her wonderful daddy was gray-haired and distinguished. They were all together, and it had been the best day ever.

An act came up on the stage, a beautiful woman in a sparkly leotard. She carried a small stand that held knives in a semi-circle, like an open fan. The blades glinted in the sunlight and looked sharp and dangerous.

A tall man wearing tails and a white vest walked to the platform and announced his act.

"What's he doing, Daddy?" Pro asked her father.

"It's called 'the Bally,' pumpkin," her father said. He always called her 'pumpkin' and she loved it.

The man on stage talked about skills and other things, but Pro didn't listen. She was too busy looking from her dark mother to her light father and back. She was so happy to spend time with both of them, and it had been so rare they did things together anymore. Pro had heard them arguing at night, and it always scared her.

There was a strange noise, like a 'thwack.'

Her eyes turned to the stage. The sparkly woman stood against the red-painted background, her body in front of the circle target. There was the hilt of a knife sticking out of the wood an inch or two from her nose.

The man picked up a second knife from the holder, and with a quick move, threw it at the woman.

Pro gave a little shriek as the second knife hit the wood inches from the woman's cheek with another resounding 'thwack.'

Her father took her hand and brought it to his lips and kissed it. "Don't worry, pumpkin, this guy knows what he's doing."

Rapidly, the man in the tailcoat grabbed the knives from the holder and threw them around the body of the sparkly lady, coming close enough to make Pro jump, but never hitting her.

After he threw all the knives, Pro relaxed. Then the sparkly lady pulled the knives from the wood as the tailcoat man pulled out a strip of black velvet cloth. As she reloaded the stand with the knives, the man covered his eyes with the cloth as a blindfold.

Once the knives filled the holder again, he turned to face the target. The woman kept one knife with her, and she stood against the wooden background. She tapped the knife she held against the wood, and instantly the man threw his knife, striking the place the woman had indicated.

She did it a second time, and the knife hit the wood where she had tapped. They did it again and again until all the knives were stuck in the panels. Then she came forward as he removed the blindfold, and together they took a bow.

Pro applauded madly, relieved that the sparkly lady wasn't hurt. She looked at the indentations on the back of the target where the tailcoat man had thrown the knives.

And it all came together in her mind.

She jumped up in bed, fully awake. Shaded sunlight behind tall buildings shone through the windows of the guest room at her mother's apartment and Pro stared at the clock which read 7:00.

She was due at the precinct in less than an hour!

With a cry, she headed to the bathroom and frantically showered and groomed. She kept her tresses in a short cut, which helped speed things up. But, because of the kinkiness of her hair, she skipped washing it this morning. It would take too much time to brush it, and if wet, that process would be torture.

She dressed in a simple white shirt and dark pants, put on her black sneakers from the previous day, and was ready by 7:25.

Her mother, who didn't have to leave for her own job for an hour, handed Pro a Styrofoam cup of coffee as she rushed for the door.

"How did it work out with that young man last night?" she asked as Pro undid the locks on the apartment door.

Pro paused at the open door for a moment. "Oh, pretty good. I arrested him!"

And she was gone.

Elisha shook her head. "I am never gonna get grandchildren."

She arrived at the precinct, dressed in her uniform as fast as she could, and headed upstairs for roll call. Her assignment with Terrell would be desk duty that day, something that was required of all uniformed officers at least once a month and sometimes once a week. However, she had a feeling the excitement would be at the precinct once she got a chance to talk to the detectives.

At the morning meeting, Pro requested to be assigned to the main reception desk. Terrell gave her a dirty look, as this was a place most cops avoided. You ended up dealing with the public and answering a lot of questions while telling people to wait.

"Pro, why'd you ask for that duty?" Terrell complained in a low voice.

"I want to see Chu and Franks the minute they arrive," she offered.

Terrell shook his head. "So why should I suffer?"

Once the roll call meeting had ended and the officers left the conference room, Terrell and Pro headed out to sit at the two chairs on the main desk.

At five minutes to ten, in the door came Chu, dressed in a dark suit and reading a file as he walked. Behind him was Franks, who gave a nod to Pro.

"Detectives?" Pro called and gestured them over.

Chu glanced up, saw Pro and paused. "Officer?"

"Sir, I think I know who killed Mick Wexler."

Chu and Franks drew close to the desk and whispered.

"How?" Franks whispered.

"What proof do you have?" Chu insisted.

"If you can show me the crime scene photos, I think I can explain."

Chu appeared doubtful, and he turned to Franks. Franks shrugged, and murmured, "Couldn't hurt to look."

Pro glanced at Terrell, who just said, "Go! I got you covered."

Pro walked up to the second floor with the pair of detectives. The bullpen was much busier during the day than it had been the previous night. Most of the desks had people at them, some talked on the phone loudly; some were in a heated conversation with their partner; one man was typing away at a computer using only two fingers.

Chu pulled out the folder of photos at his desk and settled into the seat. "Okay, impress me."

Pro pulled out the photo of the framed plywood sheet. "You see the marks on the plywood?"

Chu grumbled, "Yeah, we talked about those last night, so what?"

"My parents took me to a carnival when I was a kid. There was a knife thrower doing his act. His knives made the same marks on the wooden background as these. Plus the knife used to stab Wexler? It was a throwing knife, like those used in that kind of act."

Franks frowned. "You thinking it was that guy — Todd Dagger?"

Chu shook his head. "We questioned him. His girlfriend alibied him for the time of the murder."

"Well, I found out some other things," Pro offered. "It turns out Wexler was a big one for stealing acts... and girlfriends."

Franks shook his head. "I'm not following."

Pro went on. "What if Wexler was learning a knife act and was getting help?"

The two detectives stared at her blankly.

Pro exhaled sharply. "I mean, the guy had to have someone to throw the knives around, right? And not every lady would be up for that. I mean, I wouldn't do it."

Both detectives looked at each other, and a wide grin appeared on Chu's face.

Franks turned to Pro. "That's some good thinking, officer."

Chu went through papers in their file. "We have contact information for both Dagger and the woman, right?"

"Camila," Pro blurted, as the detectives turned to her in surprise. Pro shrugged and added, "I saw them last night."

Franks looked very pleased. "You hear that, Tom? Our rookie here saw them last night and could give us the names off the top of her head."

This seemed to annoy Chu. "Okay, okay, you've got good instincts, officer. So, let's get Camila and Dagger in here and question them separately."

Franks smirked. "And see if their alibis hold up."

"My partner and I could make the bust, sir," Pro urged excitedly.

Chu frowned. "Aren't you and Officer Hodges on desk duty today?"

Pro sighed. "Yes, sir."

Franks gave out a bellowing laugh. "Cool your jets, officer. I promise we'll bring you up once they're here."

"Provided the front desk can spare you," Chu teased.

Both detectives headed downstairs to talk to the dispatcher, and Chu pulled his cell phone. Pro guessed he was calling the DA to get a search warrant.

She headed back to the front desk and her partner.

It was several hours later that Pro saw Chu and Franks arrive back at the precinct. They were escorting Todd Dagger, who was in handcuffs and glowering.

They were followed by a pair of uniformed officers who brought in Camila. The woman did not look pleased, and even fearful.

The group headed up to Interrogation, and Terrell turned to Pro. "Go ahead."

"What?" Pro asked, hopefully.

"You wanna go up there, I can tell. It's okay, I got this covered."

She clambered up the steps to see the uniformed officer heading back down the stairs. She approached Chu and Franks and asked, "How did it go?"

"Found Wexler's cell phone at Dagger's place," Chu said with a smile. "They turned it off so we couldn't track it."

Frank piped up. "Found some interesting texts between Wexler and Camila once we turned it on. There were also lot of calls to the burner phone Camila had in her purse."

Chu took over. "We're going to work on them now. You wanna watch?"

"Yes, sir, I do."

"Stay on the far side of the one-way mirror, and you can go look in from room to room and listen at the speakers."

So Pro did.

She started by observing Chu with Todd Dagger. He asked a few questions and then built a strong narrative, one that sounded sympathetic to Dagger. Chu was acting as if he was on the knife-thrower's side. After all, a friend attempted to steal his act and his girlfriend betrayed him by helping.

Todd had a deep voice, and he said little except to deny he'd done it again and again.

Pro turned the sound down on the one speaker, then walked over to listen in on Franks with Camila. Franks threatened the young woman with jail time as an accomplice because she offered an alibi to Dagger.

Franks spoke quietly, but with intensity. "You'd better tell me the truth, because if you go down as an accomplice to murder one, you are going away for a long time."

This broke Camila quickly. She rapidly denied that Todd had been with her the night of the murder. Soon, she confessed that she and the deceased had been lovers with a plan to take Todd Dagger's jobs and do them together. She claimed Dagger was taking advantage by keeping most of the money after she booked most of the work. Finally, with tears that appeared forced to Pro, she admitted she told the detectives Todd was home because she feared for her life.

As an officer took Camila's statement to write it up and get her signature, Franks went over and joined Chu.

Pro dutifully walked over and raised the volume on the other speaker.

"Hey there, Mr. Dagger," Franks said as he stepped into the room. "I just had a long talk with your lady friend."

Franks then told Dagger that Camila confessed to lying about his whereabouts because he'd told her to do it.

That was all it took for Todd Dagger.

The big man went off on a long rant about how "that bastard" working with his "useless bitch" had stolen from him. He complained that the fool woman was teaching the upstart his act that he'd created from scratch.

"But in the end, I took care of him," Dagger boasted.

The detective's use of simple techniques had impressed Pro. She shook her head, appreciating that both Franks and Chu made it look so very easy.

Franks and Chu left the room as uniformed officers wrote up both their statements and booked and processed the knife-thrower. They stood next to Pro and watched the suspect through the one-way glass.

Pro finally gathered the courage to speak to the detectives. "I must tell you, you both are great at questioning a suspect."

Franks' lip curled up in a small grin. "Well, I've been doing it a long time."

Chu chuckled. "And this pair was pretty easy. When we picked them up, I could sense the tension, so we just played them against each other."

"The surprise in this case," Franks gloated. "Is that you have a good head for this stuff, officer."

Pro blushed. "Thank you, sir. I want to be a detective." She glanced over at Chu. "I mean, when I'm ready."

Franks shook his head. "Some people are more ready than others, officer." He now looked over at his partner. "And sometimes when an opportunity comes, take it."

Chu sighed. "What my partner is trying to tell you in his own clumsy way is that he is retiring in about a month."

Franks snickered. "And what my partner is trying to say, in his even clumsier way, is that he might like to have you as his new partner."

Pro's mouth fell open, and she turned to Chu, fighting the urge to jump up and down in joy. "Really?"

Chu put his hands up in a calming gesture. "We have to run it by the Captain…"

"Oh, of course," Pro reasoned, trying to control her beating heart.

Franks continued, "And it's gonna be a lot of work. A lot of extra hours riding with us and learning the ropes. And you'll have to learn fast."

"Yes, sir."

Chu confirmed, "But you will get our highest recommendation. The job's yours if you want it."

"And if you don't crap out," Franks concurred.

"My answer would be, yes sir," Pro said.

The huge smile on her lips was dazzling.

6. The Prestige

"So, you are going to be a new detective!" Jamie exclaimed.

"A new *homicide* detective," Pro answered. "I can't believe it, this is what I always wanted."

"You're amazing," Jamie told her as he poured the last glass of wine from the now empty bottle.

They were sitting on Pro's sofa in her small apartment in Brooklyn. The worn coffee table in front of them had several types of food in styrofoam containers, and the pair of them had sampled the different delicacies.

Pro had called Jamie right after work and told him the news, and he offered to bring food and wine to celebrate. But she certainly had not expected him to show up with two bagfuls of different choices. There was falafel, hummus, and baba ganoush; then a container of General Tso's Chicken and brown rice; finally a serving of Fish and Chips, with a bottle of malt vinegar and a plastic squeeze bottle of catsup.

When Jamie arrived carrying the bags of food, it shocked Pro. "This is enough for a week!"

"Then you won't have to go shopping," Jamie laughed. "It's okay, I did well with shows during lunch hour on Wall Street today."

"Still doing street shows?"

"Aye, for another month."

Pro frowned. "Why only that long?"

"Pro, my visa will be up. I have to go back to Ireland."

They chatted about other things as they ate, but she brought the realization up that Jamie would have to leave several times.

"Can't you extend your visa?" Pro asked.

Jamie shook his head sadly. "I have to leave the country to do that, and the immigration laws are pretty tight right now. Besides, I have responsibilities…"

"Oh crap! You're not married, are you?" Pro babbled.

This made Jamie fall into gales of laughter, which annoyed Pro even more.

He took her hand in his and said, "No, darlin'. It's me parents. They need help, and I'm their only son."

Pro flushed. "O-of course."

And with a look of compassion and wonder, he brought his lips to hers.

And it happened again.

Electricity, fire, desire, moving up and down her spine to make her tingle in all the right places.

She broke the kiss and stood, much to Jamie's surprise.

"Let's…um…get the food in the kitchen."

Jamie stood as well. "Why?"

"Because this sofa turns into a bed."

The speed with which Jamie cleaned off the table and got the food in the fridge was impressive.

While he did that, she moved the coffee table to the corner and opened the bed. She also went to two large glass tubes that contained candles. She looked at them for a moment. There was actually dust inside the glass, since she'd only last lit them the last time she'd made love with Julius Trent, her lover at the academy. She took a long-stemmed lighter and pulled the trigger to start the flame and light the candles.

She threw her shoes in the closet and lay out on the bed, many emotions running through her. She was glad she had taken the time to change into a clinging, silken dress. It would be easier to remove.

Jamie came out from the kitchenette, saw Pro on the bed, and quickly joined her. They kissed again, and soon his shirt was off, and it was true, the dress was easy to remove.

Both of them breathed heavily, as articles of clothing fell away, and then hands touched sensitive parts, while lips nuzzled erogenous zones.

Her mother had been right, the magician was excellent with his hands and his fingers possessed unexpected talents.

They moved, caressed and rubbed, as Pro felt her breath catch in her throat and her body shudder under his expert manipulations.

Soon they were both naked, and she lay back as he rested on top of her.

"I'm a bit…uh…nervous," she gasped.

"I find it hard to believe you could be nervous about anything, *Storeen*," Jamie whispered.

"What does that mean?"

"It's Gaelic. It means 'my little treasure.'"

"Oh, that's nice," she sighed. "Love me, Jamie."

Kissing her passionately, he slowly joined his body with hers. This caused delightful moans to escape from Pro's lips as a wave of sensations surged through her. The ecstasy that burned within her made her wonder why she had avoided this experience for so long.

Jamie moved within her, causing squeaks and moans to escape her lips. She flipped them over so that she was on top, straddling him. Both of them gasped as her hips gyrated against his, wild and uncontrolled. As her pace increased, both of them reaching for fulfillment. Their passion built until they surrendered to a sweet release, giving in to the pleasure that consumed them both.

She lay back on the bed, dizzy from the rush of emotions and the physical exertion.

They lay in each other's arms, trying to recover from the amazing experience.

"Can you stay?" Pro gulped.

"Ah, sure, what time do you have to leave in the morning?"

"7:00 AM."

"Then," Jamie wheezed, "We better get up at 6:00 if we want to do this again."

And they did.

One month later, Jamie and Pro sat in the outer area of Laguardia Airport, just outside the security line.

"I'll have to go soon. It might take an hour to get through that," Jamie stated glumly with a look at the crowd of people going through the line.

"Just another minute or two," Pro said, gripping Jamie's hand. She was biting her lip to stop any tears from coming, but it was a struggle.

For the last month, Jamie had stayed with Pro, and they spent all of her non-work time together. It had been tricky as the captain had approved Pro's promotion, and she had to put in a lot of extra hours to learn the new job.

But Jamie was there every night, to rub her feet or offer a glass of wine.

And to make love.

She had never had a relationship where the sex was steady, yet the Irish man was very inventive at the same time.

They never spoke of love. With him leaving, it was best that neither of them brought it up. But Pro had to admit, she'd fallen for the man.

"Thanks for going out to dinner with my Momma. I wanted her to meet you."

"She's a delight," Jamie said, and rubbed her fingers over their clenched hands.

The tears began to fall, and Jamie lifted her chin. "Please don't cry, Pro."

"I can't help it," she sniffled. "But that's what I get. I know that magicians always leave."

"I'm sorry."

"No, you're not!" she sobbed. "You'll forget about me."

"There is nothing on this earth that could make me forget this last month, darlin'. It's been one of the best months of me life."

"Me, too," Pro replied in a small voice.

Jamie reached up and with a flick of his fingers, a white cotton handkerchief appeared at his fingertips. Pro took it and dabbed her eyes.

"Keep it," he told her, "to remember me."

The pair rose, and he began to walk toward the line with Pro beside him.

"Now, you go back to your city, and become the best damn detective New York has ever seen," Jamie demanded.

"And you go become famous so you can travel the world," Pro suggested. But her mouth was now a tight line, her emotions pushed down.

He pulled her into a hug and whispered, *"Is maith liom tú."*

Jamie parted from her, joined the line and Pro watched him go.

Finally, she turned to head to the bus that would take her back to Brooklyn. She was convinced of three things: that Jamie had just told her he loved her in Gaelic; that she was determined to become the best homicide detective she could.

And that magicians always leave.

FREE PREVIEW

Murder
By
Misdirection

Debra Snow

MIND
BENDER
PRESS

PREVIEW

Murder By Misdirection

D etective Tom Chu sat in the driver's seat of his unmarked police car. Glancing in the rearview mirror, he moved his dark, straight hair off his forehead. He had narrow eyes that spoke of his Korean ancestry, and his slim fingers grasped the steering wheel. Since he was an expert in several forms of combat, he enjoyed the fact that he was thin and of average height. It always surprised a bigger man when his skills helped him take down a larger suspect.

He leaned his head back and closed his eyes, just as the sound of a finger ring tapping on his window caused him to raise his head and glance over.

"You takin' a nap?" the African-American woman at his window said, muffled by the closed glass.

Chu smiled, sat up, and hit the release to unlock the passenger door as his partner, Pro Thompson, came around the car. Chu reached over and opened her door as she carried two cups of coffee, the white paper emblazoned with the green Starbucks logo.

Pro got in, her gray pantsuit and white blouse giving her the look of a corporate professional. This not only hid her strong, fit body, but the shoulder holster and SIG Sauer P229 sidearm she wore.

Chu knew from his partner's workout regime that she could handle any situation a cop might face.

She handed him one cup and kept the other for herself. Chu took a sip; She prepared it just the way he liked it. That was the nice thing about having a partner: they knew your habits.

"So, were you sleeping?" Pro teased as she took a swig from her own cup.

"No, just enjoying the calm before the storm," Tom answered.

"What storm?" Pro frowned and looked out at the spring day. "There's not a cloud in the sky."

Chu looked over at his partner, her striking blue eyes in such contrast to her dark skin tone, which was the color of café au lait. "I mean the calm before our day gets busy."

"I heard that," Pro sighed and ran her free hand through her hair, which was short in the back and longer in front. It not only looked professional, but with the tight natural curl of her hair, it was a logical choice that required little care or upkeep. "But it might not get busy. We could just have a lovely spring day, sit in our car, and maybe even relax."

Tom smiled. "That would drive you crazy. You're an adrenaline junkie."

"Still, it could be a quiet day."

"Pro, we're homicide cops in New York City. Every day is crazy."

Pro looked out the windshield at the city—her city. They parked their car at a hydrant on the corner of 52nd and Ninth Avenue. She'd grown up only about thirty blocks north of here. She had to admit, the city never stopped, never slowed down, and she got a rush from being a part of it, being out there, making a difference.

Chu's cell phone rang with a very businesslike tone, and he reached under his suit jacket to pull it from his belt. "And so the craziness begins," he said, as he moved it to his ear. "Chu," he said as he hit the virtual button on his device. He looked to Pro, but she had already retrieved her detective notebook from her pocket and pulled out a pen. "258 West 47th Street? We're on our way."

Chu slipped the phone back into his belt and started the car all in one well-practiced move.

"We got a DB?" Pro asked, using the abbreviation for a "dead body."

"We do," Chu said as he glanced into the side mirror and slid the car into the busy traffic. "911 got a call. Uniforms got there fast. They have the DB and a suspect in custody."

Pro considered this. "That'll speed up the process. Seems like we caught an easy one."

"Yeah, it's good work when they catch the perp still at the scene," Chu agreed, as he weaved the car across several lanes to take a left turn down 46th Street.

Pro had pulled out the small rotating blue light and put it on the dashboard. Since they had a suspect in custody and traffic wasn't too bad, there was no need for sirens. As a New Yorker herself, she tried to avoid additional noise pollution in a city that was already far too loud.

They drove up 47th Street and pulled over to see an officer in front of a three-story brownstone. The uniformed man appeared younger than the mandatory twenty-one and gave the impression of a teenager playing dress-up.

The detectives came out of the car like a shot, and Pro smiled. She loved the fact that her partner moved as quickly as she did. He was the senior partner in the relationship, though he was only in his mid-thirties.

"Whaddaya got?" Chu requested as they moved toward the brownstone. Pro was happy to let her partner take the lead, though she could do so when needed. But her year of working with Tom Chu had taught her how to be a good detective fast. He would expect nothing less of her.

"Right here on the ground floor," the officer said, his Adam's apple bobbing up and down as he spoke. "Some kind of magic shop."

Pro broke into a smile. "Floss's Magic. I've been here."

Chu gave her a puzzled glance. "You have?"

"When I was a kid," Pro explained. "It's well known in the magic community. The guys who do that stuff hang out in the store all the time, usually showing each other card tricks."

Chu shrugged. "Let's see the scene."

The young officer escorted them up the short flight of stairs, and they took a left into a separate entrance next to the main door.

They passed through a door and into a storefront. There were glass display cases filled with flowers made from feathers and paper, and an enormous bouquet of what appeared to be fifty-dollar bills. Someone haphazardly repaired the cracked glass on several cases with nothing more than shipping tape.

Running up the walls on three sides were bookcases crammed with paraphernalia: there were wooden boxes with large, spotted dice resting on top of them; a small box of clear plastic filled with brightly colored silk handkerchieves; large coins of various currencies and holders to display them and possibly make them disappear.

However, the shelves had a layer of dust and all the tricks, though still impressive, looked old and dingy. The place was claustrophobic from the total amount of things that were packed in its limited space.

Standing near a red curtain to a back room was a female uniformed officer. She was average height, thin, with a strong, lithe body and short black hair under her hat. She stood at military rest, waiting for the detectives.

"Wow, this takes me back," Pro said, as her partner handed her a pair of rubber gloves. "It is exactly the same as it was twenty years ago."

"Really?" Chu said, as he pulled gloves onto his own hands. "I can't imagine you coming to a place like this."

Her mouth became a hard line. "I didn't choose it. I was a kid and brought to places like this all the time." She turned to the officer. "Tillie, isn't it?"

"Yes, ma'am." The officer smiled.

"Where's our vic?"

"Behind this counter," she told them, and stepped back so that Pro could get to the walkway Tillie had blocked with her body.

The pair of detectives looked over to see the man dead on the floor. He was older, with white hair and a pair of horn-rimmed glasses on his face. He wore cheap clothes that were worn at the elbows and knees.

"That's Albert Floss, the owner," Pro stated sadly.

"You know him?" Chu frowned.

""Yes, that case about a year ago? He was a magician at that magic club we busted."

"Right, Magic Over Manhattan. I remember," Chu replied, then turned to the uniformed officer. "Tillie, is forensics called in?"

"Yes, sir. They're coming from another scene. Going to be delayed."

"All right," Chu said and walked around the corner of the glass cabinet to crouch low near the body.

Pro leaned in. "Ligature around the neck," she noted.

Chu carefully opened the collar of the man's shirt to look at the line of red skin around his neck. He picked up a two-foot-long red rope that lay on top of the man's open vest. "Here's our murder weapon."

"Let me see," Pro said and took the end of the twisted braid in her hand. "No, this isn't it."

"Huh?" Chu replied. "It's a rope, and the marks suggest a rope was the murder weapon."

"Yes, but this is magicians soft-cut rope," Pro explained. "It would be much easier to strangle him with a real rope from a hardware store. This looks nice, but it's just foam rubber wrapped with a cloth tube."

"We'll let forensics figure it out," Chu said and rose. "Tillie, have you verified the ID?"

"Yes, sir, it's the owner, like Detective Thompson said," she replied

"Al Floss," Pro noted and shook her head as she stood. "He's been running this place for years."

"Anyone else work here?"

"Not from what I can tell, sir," Tillie answered and looked around the tight quarters. "And I doubt there would be room for two people."

"Where's the perp?"

"He's there in the back room, which is not much bigger than this one. My partner is watching him, and he's restrained."

"Good work, Tillie," Chu said. "Let's see him."

There was a battered, old red theater curtain in the doorway that possessed a faded glory. Tillie took the detectives to it and pulled it aside.

There was a male officer standing and a man in a chair with his hands fastened behind his back. The man had carefully coifed silver hair that had some black still mixed in at the top. On his face he had a mustache with a small beard, commonly called a "van dyke." With black pants, a black shirt with an open collar, and a beautiful black velvet sports coat, his outfit suggested a tuxedo. He raised his blue eyes to the detectives.

Pro gasped and Chu glanced at her, surprised by her reaction. The man slowly rose from the chair to his full height of six foot two. He brought his hands from behind his back as a pair of manacles clattered noisily to the ground behind him.

"Pumpkin!" the strange man stated joyfully. He opened his arms and took Pro into a bear hug.

This alarmed Chu enough that he released his service weapon from his holster.

"D-Dad?" Detective Pro Thompson stammered, as the two officers and her partner stared in disbelief.

To be continued

in

Murder

By Misdirection

About The Author

Halfway through college I experienced an identity crisis, joined the army and ended up stationed in Frankfurt at the 97th General Hospital.

One night in 1979, I was in a club where a beautiful girl in a silver costume belly danced through the room. I approached her in the dressing room and begged to take classes with her.

Over the next ten years, I started start my own business. My performing life grew to include cruise ships, night clubs, resorts in the Poconos and Catskills, and TV appearances. I produced an audio tape and book series with Parade Records "Let's Belly Dance!"

In 1990, I auditioned at the Taj Mahal in Atlantic City and spent two years performing with the Taj Players. It was there I met my husband, Arjay Lewis. As our lives grew together, I began transitioning into teaching the dance, and found a fulfillment I never expected.

My husband has always been a writer, and when he started publishing, I became inspired to try my hand at the romantic mystery genre. This was a perfect complement to Arjay's paranormal mysteries.

Today we truly are, partners in crime…fiction

Also From
Mindbender Press

Paranoermal Mystery
Fire In The Mind
Seduction In The Mind
Reunion In The Mind
Haunted In The Mind
Devotion In The Mind
Asylum In The Mind
Specter In The Mind
Vengeance In The Mind
Echoes In The Mind
Infection In The Mind
Justice In The Mind
Ritual In The Mind
Vanished In The Mind

Horror
The Muse
Kept In The Dark
The Vanishing
Digger

Romantic Suspense
A Study In Murder
Murder By Misdirection
Vanishing Act

NYPD Wizard Detective
The Wizards Of Central Park West
The Vampires Of Greenwich Village
The Werewolves Of Washington Square

FREE NOVELLA

VOWS

AND OTHER TALES OF THE MACABRE

For those who enjoy a good scare, here is a collection of stories designed to give you nightmares. These stories that have been published in *Weird Tales, H.P. Lovecraft Magazine Of Horror, The Ultimate Halloween,* and *Sherlock Holmes Mystery Magazine.* If you tried to get them from their original source they would cost over $20.00. But you get them for FREE by signing up for Arjay's Newsletter

VOWS: A story of devotion that extends beyond death itself.
SIREN: A Sci-Fi fantasy of a condemned prisoner lost in space.
THE DARK: A guard sees creatures in the night...are they really there?
DREAMCATCHER: A walk in the woods...but you are not alone.
THE TRAVELER: What do you do if your flight is delayed...forever?
INTO THE ABYSS: A makeup artist gets the dream job...at a price.